Dedicated to my grandchildren

*Kelly, Kristen, Matthew,
Rachael, Kimberlee, Jonathan,
Delanie, Stephen, Christina,
Linden and Amy*

Listen to my Feelings

by Ruth Reardon
Illustrated by Roland Rodegast

The C.R. Gibson Company, Norwalk, Connecticut 06856

ISBN-0-8378-2499-0
GB750

Listen to my feelings...
put your ear upon my heart,
hearing more than words
    and actions.

Listen to my feelings...
feelings are being born,
are growing,
    changing, every day
        and they are molding me.

Listen to the real me...
Listen to my feelings.

SEPARATE THE "ME"
  from what I do!
Let disapproval center only
  on my actions,
     not on me,
  so that I feel I still am loved,
     still am good,
       though you're angry, Dad, at what I did!
Then I will feel a sense of worth
  and have the strength to change my behavior—
     some of the time, at least!

LET ME BE MYSELF—
grow according to my own uniqueness.
My personality,
my talents
are not the same
as cousin Joe's.
He knows the alphabet—
well, so what!
He also spits at me
if I beat him in a race.
Comparing us will make us feel
as though we're being measured—
and we'd better "measure up!"
Let me be "me", and he be "he"
then happier we all shall be!

PEOPLE LUMP US INTO ONE—
"THE TWINS"
  but I am "me"
  and he is "he"—
  that's two!
Each one, though like the other, still unique.
Build in that sense of self.
Be sure our roots are separate.
If we're too much entangled we cannot go
  our different ways.
Relate to each of us as though we were the only one,
  without comparison...
    without expectations.
Each of us a whole,
  not just a half.
We will feel free, and to enjoy the specialness
  of being twins.

"I'M GOING TO RUN AWAY!"
I threatened.
It would have felt so scary
if you had just agreed and said:
"All right, I'll help you pack!"
Instead, you told me that you hoped
I'd change my mind,
for you would miss me very much,
and have to go find me.
I still felt very angry
but also felt secure and safe...
and decided that I'd stay!

IT'S NOT ENOUGH
that I am loved,
I have to also feel it.
Show your love in ways I understand.
Working hard for me, all day,
means nothing to me now,
but hugs and words,
especially play
give me the feeling:
I am loved.

BALLOONS MAKE ME FEEL HAPPY.
I smile, and grown-ups smile back.
Balloons are for celebrations—
*   and only "just for fun."*
They're very impractical
*   maybe that's one of the reasons we like them!*
They always go up, so we lift our heads
*   to watch.*
They tug at the strings in our hands
*   to be free.*
If one should escape,
*   sailing over the trees,*
*   a little of us goes with it.*
You like them, Mom and Dad—
*   do they make you feel like a child again?*
Do you wish you too could sail up in the sky. . .
*   just for a little while?*
The world is so worried!
Balloons lighten the serious. . .
*   just for a bit.*
You're not wasting money—
*   you're buying some smiles!*

I CANNOT "TALK SO GOOD".
You have a library of words to use.
I can only say such simple things,
      but I feel so deeply!
Because I cannot "talk so good".
Life is so new.
I look to you for understanding
      of these feelings.
Though I do not spell them out.
If you listen . . .
You'll hear them talking in my actions,
      see them in my eyes,
            and feel them . . .
                  with your heart.

I FELT SO MAD. . .
*   when Johnny grabbed my doll*
*   and pulled her arm right out!*
I tried to kick him,
*   was going to pull his hair—*
*   it would have felt really good.*
You didn't let me.
I screamed at him,
*   you made him hold the doll*
*   and help you fix the arm,*
*   then sent him to his room awhile.*
I wouldn't play with him all day!
I am not sorry I was mad.
Feeling angry is o.k.
Pulling hair is not.

REALLY, NOW,
  MUST YOU DO IT ALL,
    FOR ME?
Sure, you can dress me much more quickly—
  with the shoes on the right feet—
but watch the look of pride on my face
  after I've done it by myself.
I feel so confident.
Each step that I accomplish
  makes me feel that I can do the next!
So when you can . . .
  let me do it.
Don't even notice there's an extra button,
  or my socks are very different,
    and tell the world, while I am smiling,
      that I did it by myself!

BE GENTLE AS YOU HANDLE ME.
In fact, to see just how it feels,
     have someone yank
          your shoes and socks off
or pull your sweater—
     with a turtle neck—off so quickly
          that you almost lose a nose!
Have someone hold your wrist
     and drag you down the sidewalk,
          leaving a red mark on your wrist.
Now tell me. . .doesn't it make you feel
     as though you were only
          a "thing"?

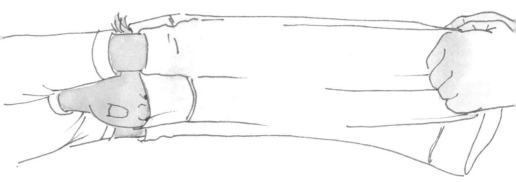

MY KITTEN DIED

I felt bad and you felt bad, too,
especially for me,
but you had the tearful funeral,
and you waited.
You could have rushed
to get another kitten—
but you waited
and let me feel the sadness,
for awhile, and talk about my loss.
I need to learn to grieve,
to feel how much I miss it
before something new
can take its place.

NOT THE OLDEST,
   NOT THE LITTLEST,
     I'm the "middlest" child!
Too young to do what the oldest does,
   too old to do what the littlest does—
     who, by the way, took my place
So what's a "middlest" to do?
What is there special,
   just about me?
Not the first—
   whatever I do has been done before.
Not the baby—
   who does cute things I sure can't
     get away with!
I feel just sort of sandwiched in!
Can you help me find something
   the others can't do or be?
So I can be proud
   of the "middlest" me?

WHEN YOU HEARD
  YOUR UNCLE JOHNNY DIED,
    you disappeared into another room.
Coming back you only smiled
  to show how strong you were.
I never saw you cry.
Is it wrong to show our feelings?
Let me see you cry,
  or I will learn to lock my tears up tightly
    where they cannot be wiped away.
Let me see you cry,
  so I can comfort you
    and feel in turn that I can cry—
      accepting comfort,
        not pretending I don't need it.

I BROKE YOUR FAVORITE LAMP—
the one you said you could never replace.
It was a special wedding gift.
You felt mad and I felt sad.
Later, you told me you forgave me.
But Mother, you keep telling others
all about it,
and reminding me, "be careful, now—
remember how you broke the lamp!"
It makes me wonder
if you really have forgiven me.
Then I feel bad...again.
Could you not talk about it anymore?
I'd think you have forgotten,
and I would feel forgiven.

NO, I DON'T WANT TO LEAVE
    my piece of blanket home.
I really don't care if my aunt
    thinks I'm still a baby!
Why do I hold on so tight—
    to a piece of ragged cloth?
When I hold it close I can feel
    that I am fine and will be O.K.
        I will be back home real soon.
In all the newness that I face,
    my blanket is familiar—
        stays the same—
            just gets a little dirtier!
After all,
    it has been through a lot
        with me—
    nights when you left me in my crib,
        times you were away,
            days my tummy felt very sick
It's a friend—
    and you don't just throw your friends away!
Let me keep it till I'm ready
    to put in a drawer
        where I can always find it
            if I need it!

IF I'M A BOY. . .OR A GIRL
I hope I do not hear you say
that when you were expecting me
you were hoping for the other.
Assure me I'm exactly what you wanted,
just as I am,
even if you had eight boys
and I'm the ninth!
To feel I disappointed you
might make me feel such guilt
that I would always try to
make it up to you,
or else resign myself
to feeling second best
all through my life.

HOW DO YOU FEEL
  when you're talking,
    and someone keeps interrupting?
When you're being talked about,
    as though you were not there?
How do you feel when you're ignored,
    or laughed at when you speak?
Or when people say
    "just go away—we're busy"?
Don't you feel you're not respected—
    that you do not really count?
Or don't those things happen
    to grown ups?. . .
Only to little ones?

WHEN I HEAR THE LATEST NEWS,
of murders, accidents, and wars—
I feel afraid inside
and wonder if I'm next!
Let me talk about it,
play it out,
ask about it. . .
after all, you do, with everyone!
Stop and listen to my feelings.
Explain, as best you can,
what's happening,
and ways that I am safe.
You cannot shield me from all the news—
but you can tell me of the good things,
of people helping people.
Let me see you planning
for some bright tomorrow,
wrapping presents for the next holiday,
or storing summer clothes
away with care,
that will make me feel
my world's not ending yet.
I will have tomorrow
and tomorrow will be happy.

WHY DON'T WE START A QUIET TIME?
Just five minutes every day.
We'll stop. . .then listen. . .
  to the hum of the refrigerator,
    the ticking of the clock,
      the sound of wind outside, the rain.
People talk about listening to birds—
  does anyone ever do it?
I feel so crowded by the noise
  that's everywhere. . .
    all the time. . .
  maybe if we stop and listen
    we can hear our thoughts
      and get to know ourselves!

I FEEL STRESS TOO—
 like everyone else,
  when you expect too much of me.
Look at your expectations.
I still am very little,
 am I ready for them?
Can you cut the list in half?
Does it really matter
 if I always wash my hands
  or always put my toys away?
The messy room will still be there
 tomorrow
  and dirty hands
   sometimes won't hurt!
Let's just sit down
 if we can find a place!
Look at a picture book and
 forget the "shoulds" and "shouldn'ts."
Don't worry—
 they'll catch up with us all
  soon enough!

WHILE YOU'RE BUSY WORKING,
*   could we talk?*
We could talk about so many things.
*   sometimes I feel so lonely*
*   when you tell me, "go and play."*
We could talk—
*   of what we did yesterday,*
*   of what we'll do tomorrow.*
I'd learn a lot and
*   I'd feel included.*
If you share your thoughts with me.

I GET A NICE, WARM FEELING
at Grandpa and Grandma's house.
I hear stories of what they did and
what you did at my age.
Bed time is late but they never tell,
breakfast is sometimes served in bed.
They never count the spoons of sugar,
always have time to read to me,
make cocoa, watch the squirrels eat.
Grandma lets me help. . .
she's getting old
and needs me.
They're glad to see me come,
and sad to see me go.
It's like another home.
But somehow I cannot wait
'till I come back home to you—
you missed me!
Things at my house seem new again.

WILL SOMEBODY CLAP FOR ME?
Early in life I lift searching eyes
   that ask—
Will somebody clap for me?
Is anyone glad that I did a good job?
That I tried?
Do you really care? Are you proud?
If you clap, the rhythm
   will bring out the best
      that is in me.
I'll feel I can do more,
   I can do better,
      because someone claps. . .
         for me.

THE LITTLE CHILD I AM TODAY
will always be within me,
sending out feelings
into my "grownup" mind.
Time and experience may seem
to bury him,
but the child will be there.
If I am now secure, feel loved,
and little hurts are healed,
in later years I'll feel down deep,
not cries of fear and pain,
but rather. . . songs.

KISS IT AND MAKE IT BETTER
when I come with a bump or a scratch,
before you say, "Oh, you're all right!"
first, let me say, "it hurts!"
Let me tell you how I feel,
unless I feel free to look at the pain,
and am able to say "it hurts!"
Later, a different kind of hurt—
of the heart—
will not get better in time.

I FEEL LIKE HUGGING MY DOG, A LOT,
because she really likes me,
just the way I am.
Doesn't care if I am clean—
she likes to lick chocolate off my face.
When I feel sad, she knows,
and snuggles close
to cheer me up.
She has no words and I have so few.
We talk with feelings.
She forgives me when I'm mad,
asks only for my love
and yes, some food, also!
She runs straight to me
right in the middle of a crowd.
She likes me and she shows it.
She is really my friend . . .
my best one!

WHEN WE'RE LAUGHING,
  giggling,
    being just plain silly,
      telling jokes,
See the funny side of me.
There is one
  even when I drive you
    "up the wall."
A sense of humor keeps us loose.
We'll not be so brittle
  that we'll break
    if we can laugh with others. . .
      and at ourselves!

I FEEL YOUR LOVE. . .
That holds me close, and makes me know
    you love me as I am. . .
        love that makes me feel that I am safe
          within your arms. . .
    a love, that though it has a note of sadness
        still holds me close
          and reaches out to meet my needs,
    although you wish they were not
        special needs.
It is a love that lives with the heartache
    of what I'll never do
        and still smiles
          when I learn something new. . .
    that thinks of what I might have been,
        but keeps enveloping
          what I am.

It is a love that gives—but more importantly
   a love that will receive my offering
      of all I am,
         which though it may not be perfect,
            is still unique.
Separates the "handicap" from the child,
   thus shielding me from all your hurt.
It is a love that learns—again—
      to smile,
         to laugh,
      to see hope and beauty
         in the love I bring to you
            and in the love I will receive.

PARENT AND CHILD—
You, the melody in tune,
  I, feeling it,
    then joining in to harmonize
until the time I find my theme,
and you add harmony.
The dance we dance
  is to all kinds of beats,
    You, leading, through the loud,
      the soft,
        the fast,
          the slow. . .
I watching,
  feeling how you move
    holding your hand,
  changing, oh so very slowly
    till we hardly notice when
      I'm dancing on my own.
As years go by,
  you'll always see in me a little
    of your song and dance.
I felt the music and rhythm
  first from you.

WHEN YOU ARE ANGRY—
   really, really angry
     at each other,
       I feel as though it's my fault.
If I'd behaved a little better
   maybe you'd be smiling at each other now?
I'm feeling worried that one of you—
   or both of you will go away!
Shall I try to fix things up—
   by being very good?
If I am not the problem
   not the cause,
     could you take a minute
      just to tell me so?
And tell me that both of you
   still love me
     and things will probably get better soon.
Maybe there will be some roses
   and apple pie
     like there was last time!

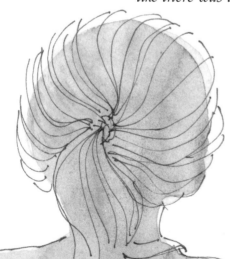

IF I COULD WRITE A LIST
of all the good things that you do,
all the help you've given,
all the love you've shown me,
it would fill a paper
about a whole mile long!
You could only write a short list
of things you "wish you hadn't."
Why is it that you think so much,
feel so badly,
about those few mistakes—
instead of being glad
about the good things?
I know I'd want to remember the long list
and forget, so very quickly,
all about the short one!
In fact,
why don't you tear it up, now?
I already have!

DECISIONS, DECISIONS, DECISIONS,
are you making every single one for me?
Am I being told what I must do, not do,
say and even feel?
How am I going to know how to live by myself?
This may come as a shock but remember. . .
you're not going to always be here!
Let me feel that I have choices.
Let me learn from those choices.
Begin now—
Which shirt should I wear. . .
blue or yellow?
Shall we walk to the park,
or the store?
Little decisions, help me feel
there's an "I" who can make them,
an "I" who lets you decide the big ones!

IS GOD ONLY IN STORIES
that happened a long time ago?
Is He living a long way off?
Or is He a part of our everyday life
so I can feel He is here right now?
If you include Him in our happy times,
ask for His help in troubled times,
let Him be real,
let Him be close,
then I'll not have to search for Him
when I am grown.

IF I'M TO GROW
I cannot always say "yes."
I have to try out "no"
  whether I mean it or not,
    to see if I can differ,
      just a bit,
        from you,
and still feel sure you love me.
My "no" is not just naughtiness—
  it's growth!

I CANNOT WAIT, MOM, DAD—
I'm growing every day—
  the years will fly so fast.
I must feel our closeness now.
Closeness where I get to know you,
  and you really, really know me,
    know my feelings.
I must feel closeness now
  if I'm to be close later on,
    and not become a stranger
      who grew up
        while you were just too busy.

IS OUR HOUSE A HAPPY HOUSE?
If it is, then it will be all right
  when bad days come,
    because the walls have absorbed the happiness.
We'll feel it there, and
  our house will smile again . . .
    tomorrow.

Designed and Illustrated by Roland Rodegast
Typeset in Palatino Italic/Roman

*My sincere thanks to Phyllis Fazzio, director of
Step One Early Intervention Program of the
South Shore Mental Health Center, my past and
present fellow staff members and all the families
in the program for all the insight they have given
me to understand, a little, the feelings of children.*